D0941196

Stolen Words

Written by Melanie Florence
Illustrated by Gabrielle Grimard

Second Story Press

She came home from school today.
Skipping and dancing. Humming a song under her breath.
Clutching a dream catcher she had made from odds and ends.
Bits of string. Plastic beads. And brightly colored feathers.
Her glossy braids danced against her shoulders.
Swaying with her. Black as a raven's wing.

Grandpa, she asked, clutching his hand,
spinning under his arm before dropping it again.
How do you say grandfather in Cree?
He stopped breathing for a moment.
A lifetime to a seven year old.

He looked down at her sadly.
I don't remember, he answered.
I lost my words a long time ago.
A frown clouded her face.
How do you lose words, Grandpa? she asked.
They took them away, he answered.
She thought for a moment.
Where did they take them? she asked.

Where they took all of us, he said.
Away from home. Away from laughter and soft words.
Away from our mothers who cried for us.
She reached for his gnarled hand.
Who took you away, Grandpa? she asked quietly.
Men and women dressed in black.
Talking to us with words we did not know, he answered.
They reached home and sat on the stairs together.

Where did they take you, Grandpa? she asked.
Away to a school that was cold and lonely,
where angry white faces raised their voices and their hands
when we used our words, he answered.
They took our words and locked them away,
punished us until we forgot them,
until we sounded like them.

Harsh sharp words.
So different from the sound of our beautiful ones.
She touched his weathered face.
Tried to wipe the sadness away
with her soft hands.

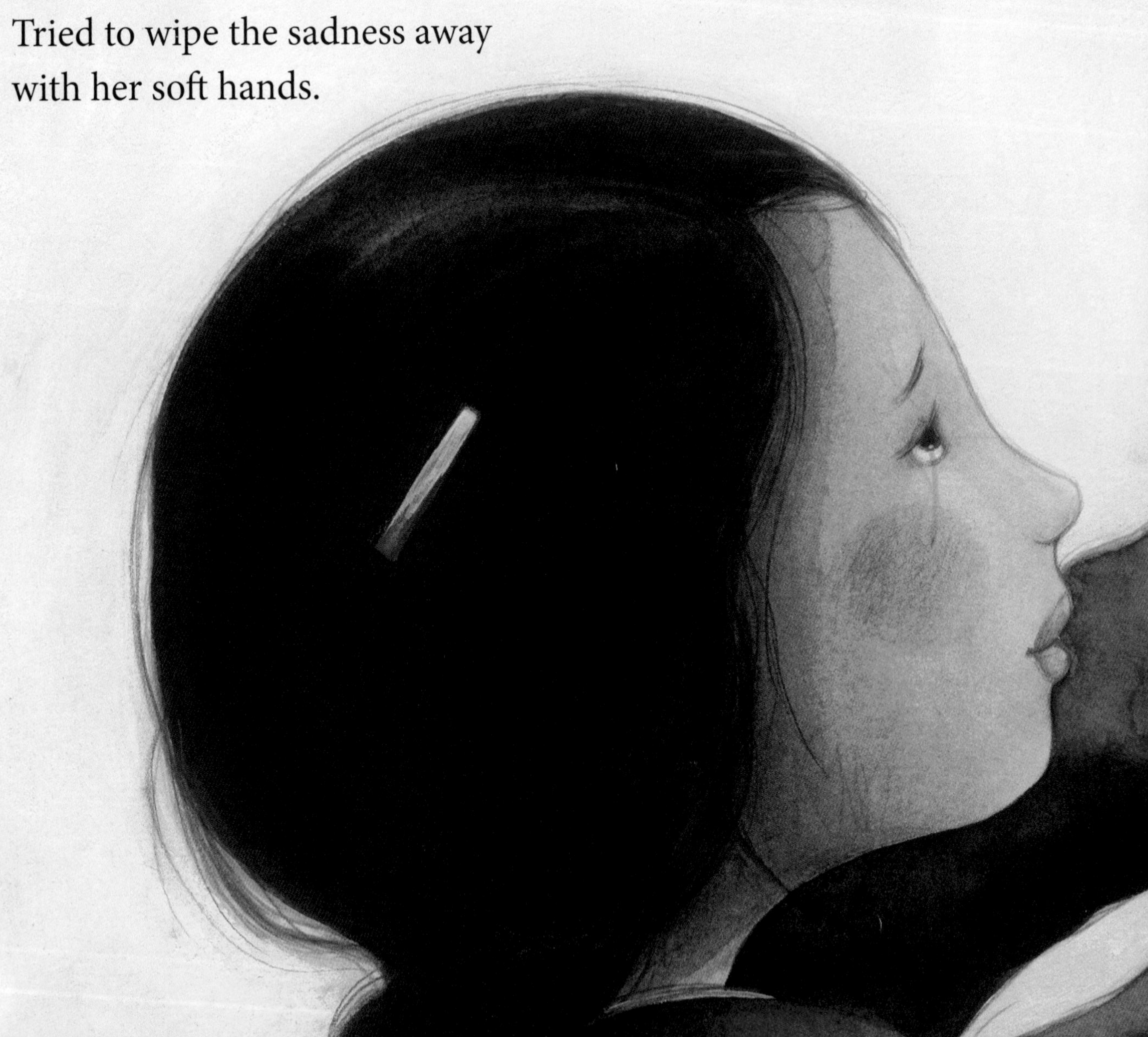

She looked down at her lap and handed him
the dream catcher that she had made for her room.
You take this Grandpa, she said.
Maybe it will help you find your words again.
He smiled at her. His granddaughter.
And touched her innocent face.
A face that had never known hard words.
Or raised hands.
He smiled and kissed her head.

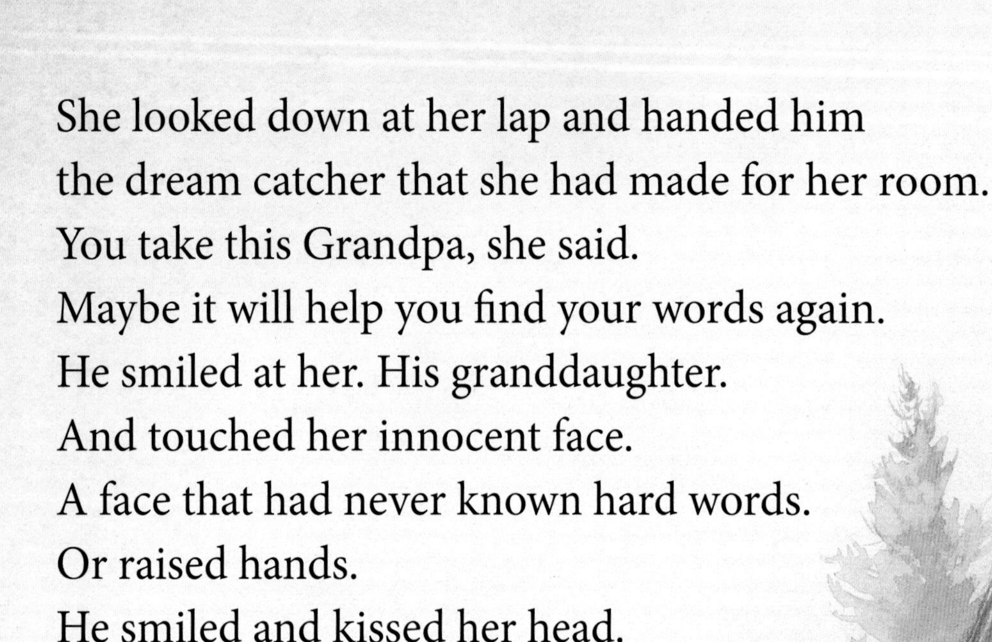

The next day, she skipped out of school again,
smiling widely at her grandfather.
She stopped in front of him and took a deep breath.
Tânisi, nimosôm, she said. His eyes widened.
She smiled brighter than the sun.
I found your words, Grandpa, she said.
She pulled a tattered well-worn paperback
out of her book bag.
Introduction to Cree, it said.

My teacher helped me find this for you at the library.
He reached for it, his hands shaking. Opened it,
feeling the soft much-loved pages under his fingers.
Nôsisim, he whispered.
Granddaughter.
The word felt familiar in his mouth.
It felt like his home. His mother.

He turned the pages of the book carefully.
Masinahikan. Book. He turned another. Word after word.
Pîkiskwêwina. His words. Pages and pages of them.
He looked at his granddaughter, his nôsisim.
Thank you. Têniki, he said.

asinahikan
nōsisim
mosom
pikiskwewina

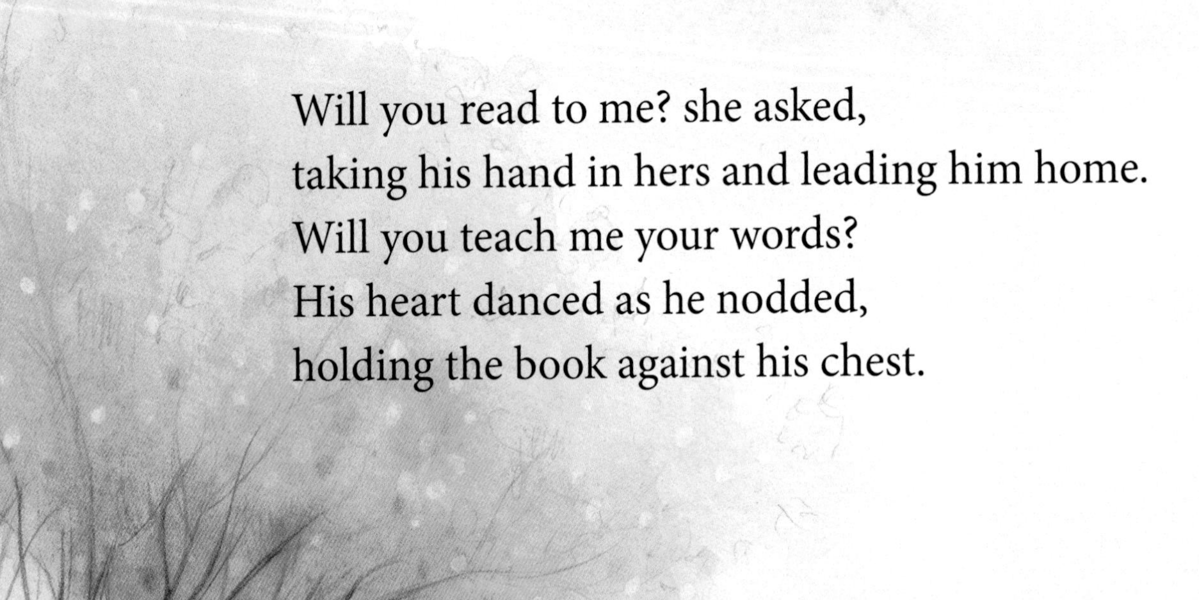

Will you read to me? she asked,
taking his hand in hers and leading him home.
Will you teach me your words?
His heart danced as he nodded,
holding the book against his chest.

For Josh, Taylor, and Chris.
And for my grandfather.
—M.F.

To my family.
—G.G.

Library and Archives Canada Cataloguing in Publication

Florence, Melanie, author
Stolen words / by Melanie Florence ; illustrated by Gabrielle Grimard.

ISBN 978-1-77260-037-7 (hardcover).—ISBN 978-1-77260-055-1 (softcover)

I. Grimard, Gabrielle, 1975-, illustrator II. Title.

PS8611.L668S76 2017 jC813'.6 C2017-902622-4

Editor/art director Kathryn Cole
Design by Melissa Kaita

Printed and bound in China

Special thanks to Arok Wolvengrey, Professor, Algonquian Languages and Linguistics and Department Head of Indigenous Languages, Arts and Cultures First Nations University of Canada

Second Story Press gratefully acknowledges the support of the Ontario Arts Council and the Canada Council for the Arts for our publishing program. We acknowledge the financial support of the Government of Canada through the Canada Book Fund.

ONTARIO ARTS COUNCIL
CONSEIL DES ARTS DE L'ONTARIO
an Ontario government agency
un organisme du gouvernement de l'Ontario

Canada Council for the Arts
Conseil des Arts du Canada

Funded by the Government of Canada
Financé par le gouvernement du Canada
Canada

Published by
Second Story Press
20 Maud Street, Suite 401
Toronto, Ontario, Canada
M5V 2M5
www.secondstorypress.ca